Words to Know Before You Read

Let's Learn The
Short
Uu
Sound

bucket
bus
Chucky
Mr. Hunter
uncle
uncover
under
unearth
uneven
until
up

www.rourkeeducationalmedia.com

Edited by Precious McKenzie
Illustrated by Marie Allen
Art Direction and Page Layout by Tara Raymo
Cover Design by Renee Brady

Library of Congress PCN Data

The Fossil Hunt / Anastasia Suen
ISBN 978-1-62169-265-2 (hard cover) (alk. paper)
ISBN 978-1-62169-223-2 (soft cover)
Library of Congress Control Number: 2012952769

Rourke Educational Media
Printed in the United States of America,
North Mankato, Minnesota

rourkeeducationalmedia.com
customerservice@rourkeeducationalmedia.com • PO Box 643328 Vero Beach, Florida 32964

The Fossil Hunt

Counselor Omar Counselor Esme Mr. Hunter

George Nadia Addie Chucky Wendy

Written By Anastasia Suen
Illustrated By Marie Allen

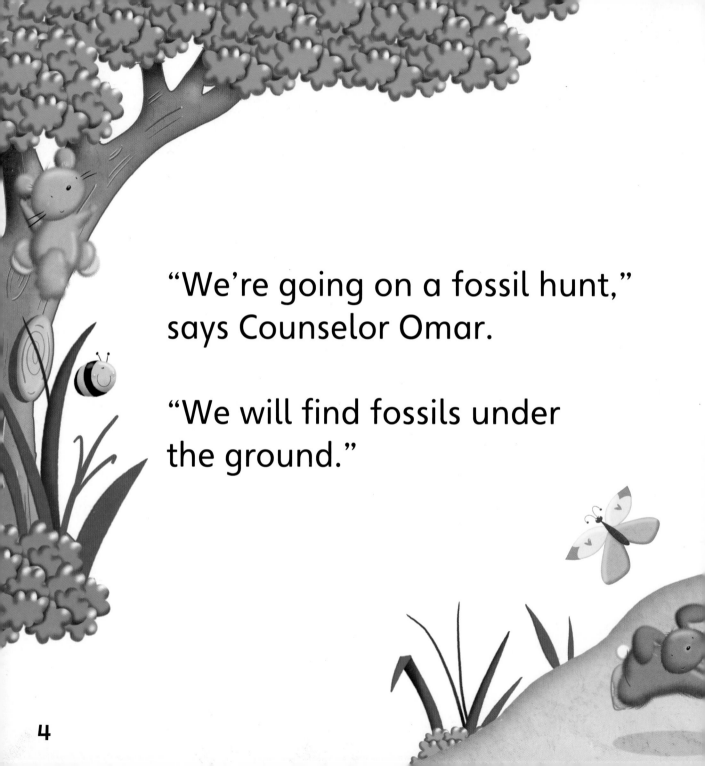

"We're going on a fossil hunt," says Counselor Omar.

"We will find fossils under the ground."

5

"Put on your seat belts," says Counselor Esme.

The bus bumps up and down. The road to the quarry is uneven.

"Look at all the rocks!" says George.

"How will we uncover the fossils?" asks Wendy.

Camp Adv

"You will need these to unearth the fossils," says Mr. Hunter.

He gives each camper a hammer and a bucket.

"Look for these fossils," says Mr. Hunter.

"They lived under the sea long ago."

"The sea?" asks Addie. "How did they get here?"

"All of this land was deep under water long ago," says Mr. Hunter.

14

"I don't see any fossils," says Chucky.

"My uncle found fossils here," says Nadia. "I will too."

"Hit the rock with your hammer," says Counselor Esme.

"That will uncover the fossil," says Counselor Omar.

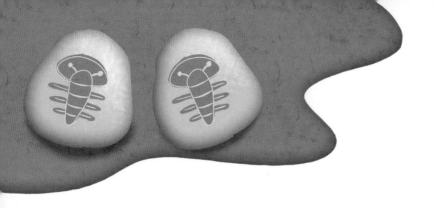

Wendy hits the rock until it cracks.

"I found fossils!"

After Reading Word Study

Picture Glossary

Directions: Look at each picture and read the definition. Write a list of all of the words you know that have the short *Uu* sound. Remember to look in the book for more words.

bucket (BUH-kit): A container that holds things. It can be plastic, metal, or wooden.

bus (BUHSS): A really large vehicle that has many seats for passengers.

Chucky (chuh-KEE): Chucky is usually a nickname for Charles.

under (UHN-dur): To be underneath or below something.

uneven (uhn-EE-vuhn): An uneven surface is not flat.

up (UHP): To move from a low place to a higher place.

About the Author

Anastasia Suen lives with her family in Plano, Texas. She started collecting rocks when she was a child, but she hasn't found any fossils yet. Maybe next time!

Ask The Author!
www.rem4students.com

About the Illustrator

Marie Allen has had an interest in art from a young age. Art was always her favorite subject in school. She loves to create bright, fun characters for children.